Ladybird  Readers

Anansi Helps a Friend

Series Editor: Sorrel Pitts
Text adapted by Sorrel Pitts
Illustrated by Barbara Vagnozzi

LADYBIRD BOOKS

UK | USA | Canada | Ireland | Australia
India | New Zealand | South Africa

Ladybird Books is part of the Penguin Random House group of companies
whose addresses can be found at global.penguinrandomhouse.com.
www.penguin.co.uk   www.puffin.co.uk   www.ladybird.com

Penguin
Random House
UK

First published 2016
003

Copyright © Ladybird Books Ltd, 2016

The moral rights of the author and illustrator have been asserted.

Printed in China

A CIP catalogue record for this book is available from the British Library

ISBN: 978-0-241-25409-7

Ladybird Readers

Anansi Helps a Friend

Picture words

Monkey

Rat

arrow

rope

Anansi the spider

Snake

children

Anansi the spider has got many small children.

Anansi's children like playing games.

The little spiders
meet Monkey.

"Can we play with your
children?" they ask.

"No!" says Monkey.
"We don't like your
father's games!"

The little spiders go
to see Rat.

"Can we play with your
children?" they ask.

"No!" says Rat.
"We don't like your
father's games!"

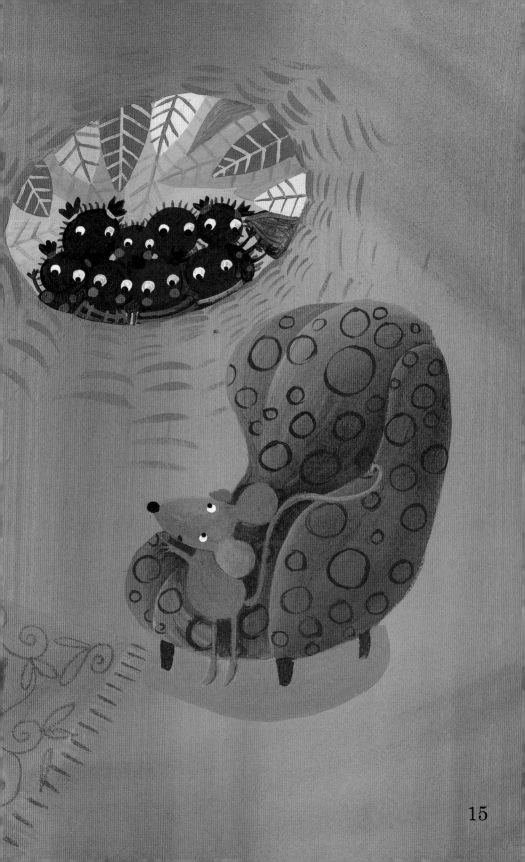

The little spiders
go back to Anansi.

"Rat's children can't play
with us," they say. "They
don't like your games!"

17

One day, Anansi and his children see Snake. There is an arrow in his body.

"We can help you, Snake,"
says Anansi.

Anansi and his children
put a rope on the arrow.

"Now pull the rope," says Anansi. They pull and pull and pull . . . and they pull the arrow from Snake's body.

Rat and Monkey and
their children watch
Anansi and his children.
They see them help Snake.

Now, Monkey's children and Rat's children can play with Anansi's children!

Activities

The key below describes the skills practiced in each activity.

Spelling and writing

Reading

Speaking

Critical thinking

Preparation for the Cambridge Young Learners Exams

Look and read.
Put a or a in the box.

1  This is Anansi the spider.

2  This is Monkey.

3  This is Snake.

4  This is an arrow.

5  These are Rat's children.

2 Circle the correct sentence.

1
a This is Rat. *(circled)*
b This is Cat.

2
a This is an arrow.
b This is a long snake.

3
a This is a big spider.
b This is a long rope.

4
a These are Anansi
   the spider's children.
b These are Snake's
   children.

5
a Snake is on the rope.
b Snake is in the tree.

3 Look at the pictures. Look at the letters. Write the words.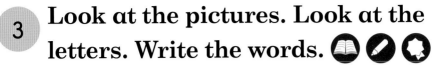

1 oMneyk

M o n k e y

2 spdire

....

3 Sanek

....

4 worra

....

5 tRa

....

4 Work with a friend. Look at the picture. Ask and answer *How many?* questions.

Example:

How many spiders can you see?

I can see eight spiders.

5 **Read the text. Choose a word from the box. Write the correct word next to numbers 1—5.**

children   games   my   We   your

I live with ¹ _my_ brothers and sisters. ² _____ want to play with Monkey's children. But Monkey says, "No! We don't like

³ _____ father's games!"

We go to see Rat. We want to play with Rat's ⁴ _____. But Rat says, "No! We don't like your father's

⁵ _____ !"

6 **Look and write *can* or *cannot*.** 📖 ✏️

1 "We ⸻ can ⸻ help you, Snake," says Anansi.

2 Snake ⸻ pull the arrow from his body.

3 Anansi and his children

⸻ pull the rope.

4 Monkey and his children

⸻ see the spiders help Snake.

5 Now, Monkey's children and Rat's

children ⸻ play with Anansi's children.

7 **Ask and answer questions about the picture with a friend.** 🗨

Rat and Monkey and their children watch Anansi and his children. They see them help Snake.

Example:

> What color is Snake?

> Snake is orange.

8 **Work with a friend. Ask and answer questions about Anansi.** ❓💬

1 *Why can't Monkey's and Rat's children play with Anansi's children?*

Because Monkey and Rat don't like Anansi's games.

2 Is Anansi nice to Snake? Why?

3 What do Monkey and Rat think about Anansi now?

4 Are Anansi's children happy now?

9 **Match the two parts of the sentence.**

"We can help you, Snake," says Anansi.

Anansi and his children put a rope on the arrow.

1 Anansi wants to

2 Snake has got

3 Anansi and his children

4 Anansi and his children pull

5 They pull the arrow from

a put a rope on the arrow.

b the rope.

c help Snake.

d Snake's body.

e an arrow in his body.

10 **Work with a friend. Look at the picture. Ask and answer *Who?* questions.** ⬤

"We can help you, Snake," says Anansi.

Anansi and his children put a rope on the arrow.

Example:

> Who has got the arrow in his hands?

> Anansi has got the arrow in his hands.

> . . . is very long?

> . . . is pulling the rope?

> . . . has got an arrow in his body?

> . . . is a big spider?

11 **Write the questions.** 📖 ✏️

(is) (Where) (Anansi)   (?)

1 Where is Anansi?

(Rat) (What) (see) (does) (?)

2 ....

(with) (Who) (play) (can) (us) (?)

3 ....

(Monkey) (like) (Does) (Anansi now) (?)

4 ....

(Where) (children) (are) (the) (?)

5 ....

12 **Circle the correct picture.**

1 Who likes playing?

a 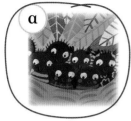   b

2 Who plays in trees?

a    b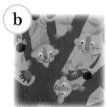

3 Who lives in a very small house under the tree?

a 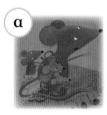   b

4 Who has got long children?

a    b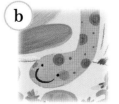

13 **Look and read.**

Write yes or no.

The little spiders go
to see Rat.

"Can we play with your
children?" they ask.

1 Rat and his children
are eating.   ......yes......

2 Rat is sitting on a chair. ....

3 Rat's children are
sitting on the floor.   ....

4 Anansi is watching
Rat and his children.   ....

5 Rat's children can
see the spiders.   ....

14 Ask and answer the questions about the picture with a friend. 🗨

Now, Monkey's children and Rat's children can play with Anansi's children!

1 Who likes Anansi now?

Monkey, Rat, Snake, and their children like Anansi now.

2 Who can Anansi's children play with now?

3 Who has not got an arrow in his body now?

4 Who is pulling the rope?

15 Circle the correct word.

"Now pull the rope," says Anansi. They pull and pull and pull. . . and they pull the arrow from Snake's body.

23

1 **Who** / **What** is in the tree?

2 **What** / **Where** is in Snake's body?

3 **Is** / **Are** Monkey and his children watching?

4 **Is** / **Are** Anansi helping Snake?

5 **What** / **Who** are Anansi's children doing?

16 **Look at 15 again and read.**
Put a ✓ or a ✗ in the box. 📖 ✿

1 Can you see Anansi? ✓

2 Can you see eight children? ☐

3 Can you see Monkey? ☐

4 Can you see Rat? ☐

5 Can you see a rope? ☐

17 Find the words. 📖

(Anansi)   Monkey   Rat   Snake

tree   children   rope

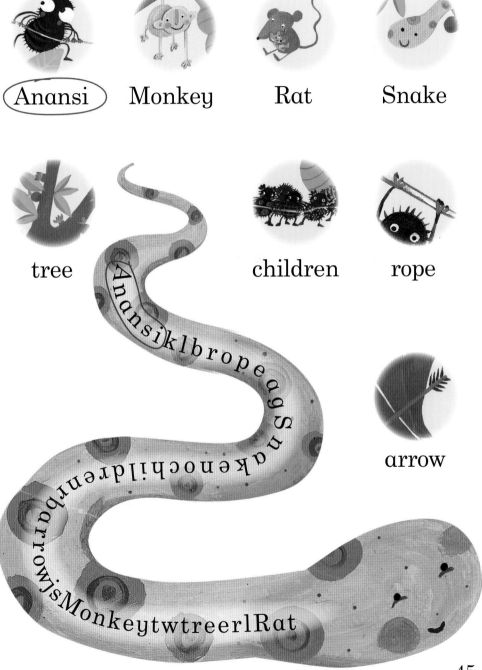

arrow

45

18 **Write the correct name.**

 Snake   Monkey   Anansi

Anansi's children   Rat

1 He has got eight legs and lots of children.   ......Anansi......

2 He lives in trees with his children.   ....

3 He is very small. He does not live in trees.   ....

4 He is very long.   ....

5 They have got eight legs, too.

46

19 Circle the correct sentence.

The little spiders meet Monkey.

"Can we play with your children?" they ask.

1 **a** Monkey's children are purple.

 b Monkey's children are yellow.

2 **a** Anansi's children are spiders.

 b Anansi's children are not spiders.

3 **a** Anansi's children do not want to play with Monkey's children.

 b Anansi's children want to play with Monkey's children.

4 **a** "Can we play with your children?" they ask.

 b "Can we play in your tree?" they ask.

Level 1

Anansi Helps a Friend

978–0–241–25409–7 ☐

Cinderella

978–0–241–25407–3 ☐

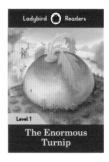

The Enormous Turnip

978–0–241–25408–0 ☐

On the Farm

978–0–241–25413–4 ☐

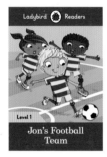

Jon's Football Team

978–0–241–25411–0 ☐

The Magic Porridge Pot

978–0–241–25406–6 ☐

In the Garden

978–0–241–26220–7 ☐

Fun with Old Things

978–0–241–26219–1 ☐

Peter Rabbit Goes to the Island

978–0–241–25415–8 ☐

Topsy and Tim Go to the Zoo

978–0–241–25414–1 ☐

Now you're ready for Level 2!

Notes
CEFR levels are based on guidelines set out in the Council of Europe's European Framework. Cambridge Young Learners English (YLE) Exams give a reliable indication of a child's progression in learning English.